# EXPLORING

# Doctor

**Peggy J. Parks**

**KIDHAVEN PRESS**™

San Diego • Detroit • New York • San Francisco • Cleveland
New Haven, Conn. • Waterville, Maine • London • Munich

Picture Credits

Cover: PhotoDisc, Inc.
© Associated Press, AP, 19
© Associated Press, Chicago Sun Times, 7
© Associated Press, Marshfield News Herald, 30
© Associated Press, Union Tribune, 29
© Annie Griffiths/CORBIS, 39
© Elizabeth Hathon/CORBIS, 25
Chris Jouan, 11
© Lester Lefkowitz/CORBIS, 16
PhotoDisc, Inc., 8, 15, 21, 26, 33, 34, 36, 37
© Roger Ressmeyer/CORBIS, 12
© Chuck Savage/CORBIS, 5

© 2003 by KidHaven Press. KidHaven Press is an imprint of The Gale Group, Inc., a division of Thomson Learning, Inc.

KidHaven™ and Thomson Learning™ are trademarks used herein under license.

*For more information, contact*
KidHaven Press
27500 Drake Rd.
Farmington Hills, MI 48331-3535
Or you can visit our Internet site at http://www.gale.com

**ALL RIGHTS RESERVED.**
No part of this work covered by the copyright hereon may be reproduced or used in any form or by any means—graphic, electronic, or mechanical, including photocopying, recording, taping, Web distribution or information storage retrieval systems—without the written permission of the publisher.

---

**LIBRARY OF CONGRESS CATALOGING-IN-PUBLICATION DATA**

Parks, Peggy J., 1951–
  Doctor / by Peggy J. Parks.
    v. cm. — (Exploring careers series)
  Includes biographical references and index.
  Contents: Different kinds of doctors—What it takes to be a doctor—What doctors do—Meet a doctor.
    ISBN 0-7377-1484-0 (hardback : alk. paper)
   1. Physicians—Juvenile literature. [1. Physicians. 2. Occupations.]
  I. Title. II. Series.
    R690 .P296  2003
    610.69'52—dc21

2002151709

---

Printed in the United States of America

# CONTENTS

**Chapter 1**
Different Kinds of Doctors         4

**Chapter 2**
What It Takes to Be a Doctor       14

**Chapter 3**
What Doctors Do                    23

**Chapter 4**
Meet a Doctor                      32

Notes                              42
Glossary                           43
For Further Exploration            45
Index                              47

CHAPTER 1

# Different Kinds of Doctors

Doctors, also called physicians, have an effect on everyone's life. They treat people when they are sick or hurt. They give advice to patients to help keep them from getting sick. They bandage knees, prescribe medicine, sew up cuts, and operate on bones. They bring new babies into the world and comfort older people who are sick or dying. Some doctors see all kinds of patients, and other doctors only see patients with a particular illness or injury. There are even doctors who never see patients at all. In the United States alone, there are over a half-million doctors. They all do different things, and they are all important in their own way.

## Family Practice Doctors

Most people have a family doctor. This is the person who sees and treats all members of the family. These doctors are usually called family practice or primary care doctors. They are trained to provide medical care to everyone from pregnant mothers to babies and adults. If their patients need further treatment, or need more specialized care, family practice doctors may refer them to a specialist.

Some family practice doctors work in large or medium-sized cities, where there are a number of hospitals and many physicians. Others, like Dr. Larry Curtis, are "country" or "rural doctors," who may be the only physician to serve an entire county of people. Country doctors work in small, rural towns such

A doctor examines a young child. Everyone, from babies to adults, needs doctors to help them stay healthy.

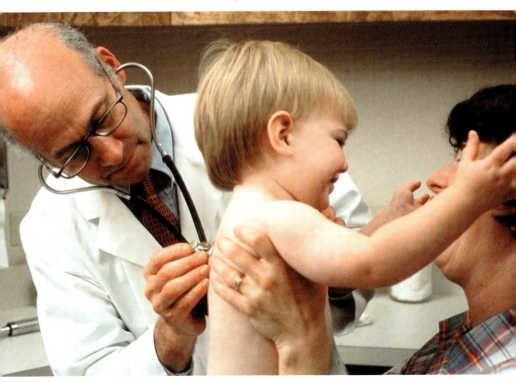

as Driggs, Idaho, where Dr. Curtis has his medical practice. He says that he enjoys being a country doctor because he feels at home in a small town and thinks of his patients as his friends. Also, he must deal with a wide variety of medical needs, as he explains: "At fall harvest, an injured farmer might not want to travel [to a distant town] for treatment. He might ask, 'Sew me up quick, doc, so I can get back to work.'"[1]

## Emergency Doctors

Many doctors have regular office hours and see most of their patients during the daytime. This is not the case, however, with emergency room (ER) doctors. ER doctors see patients at all hours of the day and night. Over 100 million people visit emergency rooms each year, for all kinds of reasons. ER doctors see patients for everything from broken bones to breathing problems, from food poisoning to pneumonia. In fact, there is no other type of doctor who sees such a variety of medical problems as an ER doctor.

Some hospitals have different types of emergency rooms—for instance, those that fly. The MCG Health System in Augusta, Georgia, has a large emergency room on the ground and a smaller one in the air. The hospital owns a specially equipped helicopter that serves as a flying emergency room. It resembles a miniature hospital ER, and it is staffed with an ER doctor and two other emergency medical professionals. When every second counts because

Different Kinds of Doctors • 7

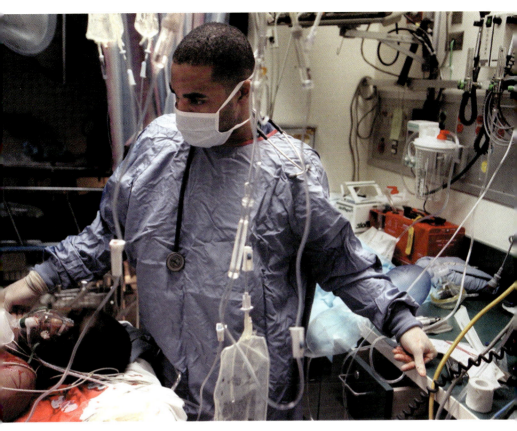

An ER doctor treats a teenage patient. Doctors who work in the ER see a variety of medical problems, from broken bones to heart attacks.

a patient is seriously ill or injured, the three jump in with the pilot and take off in the "flying ER."

## Surgeons

Doctors who perform operations are called **surgeons**. Years ago almost all surgery was performed by general surgeons. As medicine became more advanced, surgery became more specialized. Today general surgeons perform many types of common surgeries such as removal of tonsils, appendix, or breast lumps and repairing hernias. However, there are also specialist surgeons who operate only on particular areas of the body.

**Plastic surgeons** repair body parts that are abnormal in some way, from injury, disease, or birth defects. They also perform "cosmetic" surgery on patients, which is surgery that improves a patient's appearance. Several other types of surgeons include **orthopedic surgeons**, who operate on bones, joints, muscles, nerves, and tendons; **neurosurgeons** (brain surgeons) who operate on the brain and surrounding nerves; and **pediatric surgeons**, who perform surgery on children, from newborn babies to teenagers.

An obstetrician cradles a newborn baby. Obstetricians care for pregnant women and deliver their babies.

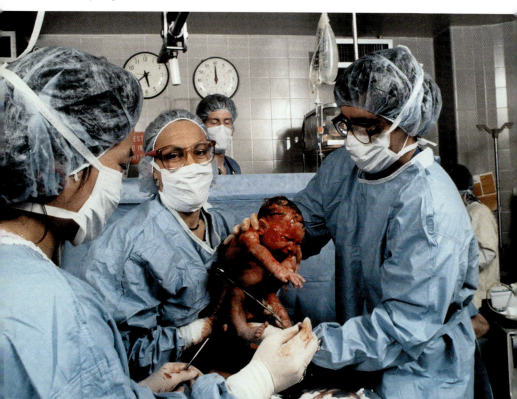

Some pediatric surgeons specialize in children's heart conditions, and are called pediatric heart surgeons. Dr. Tom Karl, of UCSF Children's Hospital in San Francisco, is a well-known pediatric heart surgeon. During the summer of 2002, Dr. Karl traveled to Nicaragua with a team of health care professionals. While he was there, he and his team performed surgery on twenty children who were born with heart defects.

## Many Different Specialties

Like Dr. Karl, many physicians specialize in treating one particular age group. **Pediatricians**, for example, work exclusively with babies, children, and teenagers. Internal medicine doctors, often called **internists**, focus on medicine for adults.

Just as some doctors specialize in a certain age group, others specialize in a particular area of medicine. **Obstetricians**, usually called OB/GYNs, are specialists in women's health. These are the doctors who take care of pregnant mothers, and who often deliver their babies. **Otolaryngologists** are doctors who specialize in problems with the ear, nose, and throat. **Dermatologists** diagnose and treat diseases of the skin, hair, and nails. Allergists specialize in treating allergies, as well as **immune system** disorders such as asthma, hay fever, and breathing problems. **Ophthalmologists** diagnose and treat eye diseases, and they perform eye surgery to correct vision problems. **Hematologists** specialize in diseases of the blood, such as sickle cell anemia and leukemia.

**Oncologists** specialize in diagnosing and treating cancer. **Anesthesiologists** give anesthesia to patients having surgery so the patients do not feel pain during the operation.

## Behind-the-Scenes Doctors

Not all doctors are involved in patient care. Instead, some perform functions that support the work of other physicians. One example is a **radiologist**, who studies and analyzes pictures taken of the inside of a patient's body. Radiology is an extremely important field, and it has been around for only about a century. Before that, doctors could only examine the outside of a patient's body, or examine the internal organs in surgery. Today, sophisticated diagnostic tests such as ultrasounds, X rays, **CAT scans**, and **magnetic resonance imaging (MRI)** allow radiologists to find internal problems before they become life threatening.

Another type of behind-the-scenes doctor is the **pathologist**. Pathologists are often called the "doctor's doctor," because they serve as scientific consultants to other physicians. They work in laboratories inside hospitals or at other locations. When doctors order diagnostic tests for their patients—such as blood samples or biopsies—it is the pathologist who analyzes and interprets those tests. Some pathologists specialize in performing examinations, or autopsies, on people who have died. These doctors are called forensic pathologists, and their work helps to determine the cause of death.

# Different Kinds of Doctors

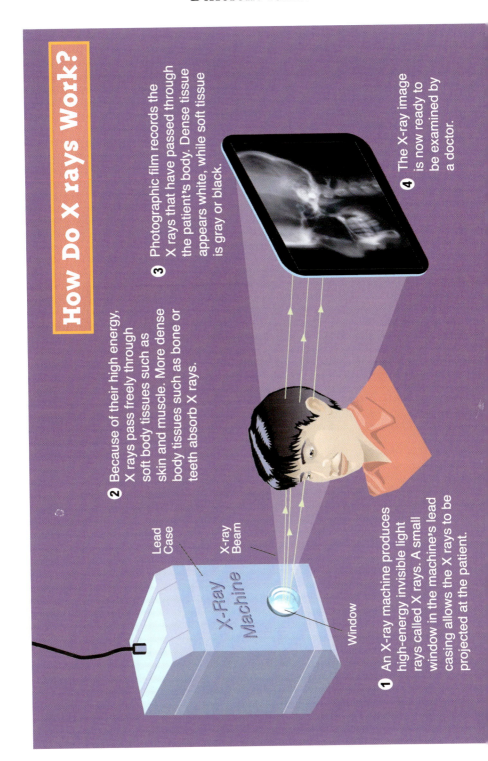

## How Do X rays Work?

① An X-ray machine produces high-energy invisible light rays called X rays. A small window in the machine's lead casing allows the X rays to be projected at the patient.

② Because of their high energy, X rays pass freely through soft body tissues such as skin and muscle. More dense body tissues such as bone or teeth absorb X rays.

③ Photographic film records the X rays that have passed through the patient's body. Dense tissue appears white, while soft tissue is gray or black.

④ The X-ray image is now ready to be examined by a doctor.

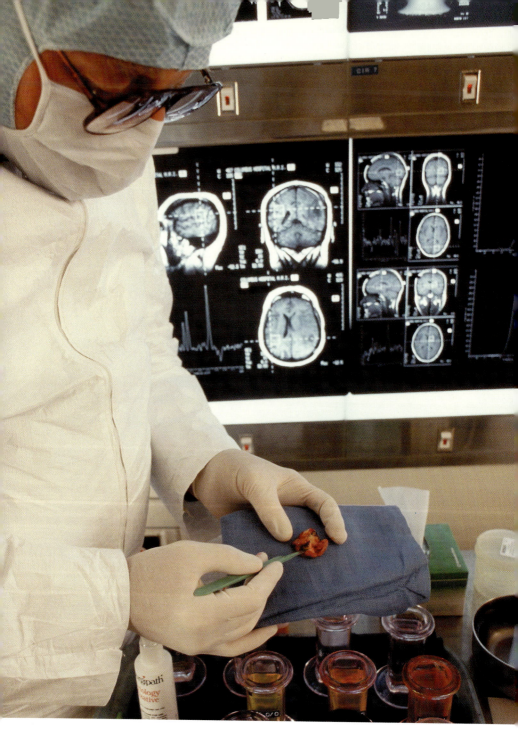

Neurosurgeons are doctors who specialize in brain surgery. Here, a doctor examines a brain tumor removed from a patient.

**Epidemiologists** are doctors whose work revolves around medical research. Often called "disease detectives," these doctors study diseases so they can figure out the cause. Epidemiologists also develop vaccines that prevent disease, as well as medicine to treat it. The work they do is extremely valuable—because of medical research, diseases such as smallpox, diphtheria, polio, and many others can now be prevented with vaccines. In the future, disease detectives may develop vaccines or cures for such serious diseases as cancer and Acquired Immune Deficiency Syndrome (AIDS). Someday they may even be able to cure the common cold—although that disease has continued to stump researchers for decades.

Doctors may work in hospitals or they may work in laboratories. Some analyze blood samples, and others deliver babies. Some doctors work with eight-year-olds, and others work with eighty-year-olds. No matter where they practice or what type of medicine they specialize in, doctors are important. Because of the work they do, people all over the world are able to live longer, healthier lives.

## CHAPTER 2

# What It Takes to Be a Doctor

People often know at a young age that they want to become doctors. Perhaps they are naturally good at math and science. Maybe they have a desire to help people and to make a difference in people's lives. Or, they may just want a job that is full of challenges. These are all very good reasons to consider a medical career. However, anyone who wants to become a doctor must understand how much work it takes to achieve that goal.

The road to becoming a doctor is a long and difficult one. In fact, doctors go through more education and training than almost any other type of professional. At the very minimum, it takes eleven years to become a doctor, and longer for highly specialized medical fields. Still, most doctors love their work and believe it was well worth the years of effort.

## The First Four Years

Aspiring doctors spend the first four years of college earning their bachelor's degrees. Many students major in what is known as "premed," which has a curriculum that is heavy in science and math. Premed students study such things as physics, chemistry, and biology, and take other advanced mathematics and science courses. During this time students often volunteer or

A premed student studies hard to become a doctor. Becoming a doctor requires more education and training than most other professions.

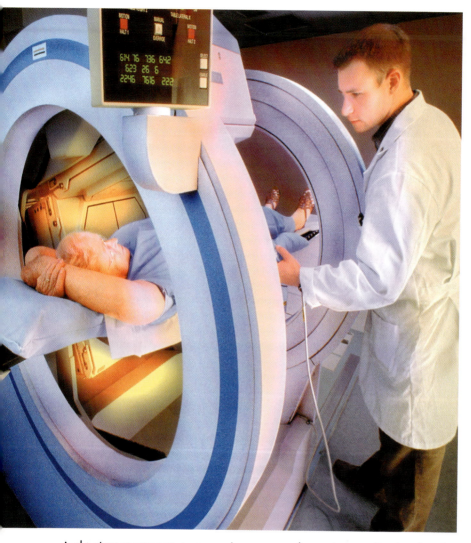

A doctor oversees a scanning procedure. In medical school, students observe and assist doctors in such procedures.

work part-time in hospitals, clinics, or doctor's offices, so they can gain knowledge and experience.

When premed students are in their third or fourth year of college, they apply to medical school. There are nearly 150 medical schools in the United States, and acceptance to these schools is highly competitive. Students must achieve a high score on an examination called the Medical College Admission Test (MCAT). They must complete an essay to explain why they want to be a doctor. Many schools require letters of recommendation. Also, the grades the students have earned in college are an extremely important consideration. Medical students almost always have grade point averages of 3.5 or higher.

## Intensive Study

Once students are admitted into medical school, they spend the first two years on what is often called "heavy book learning." They attend classes in anatomy, biochemistry, and physiology. They study pathology, medical ethics, and laws that govern medicine. They learn about the human body and how it works. They learn about disease and how the human immune system fights disease. They also study pharmacology, which is the science of medications.

During the second year, students begin to learn about basic medical tasks. This includes learning how to examine patients, how to take medical histories, and how to diagnosis certain illnesses.

## Learning on the Job

The third year of medical school is when students do their clinical rotations, which means they work with doctors and other health care professionals. They observe and assist internists, surgeons, and pediatricians, as well as radiologists, neurologists, family practice doctors, and ER doctors. This gives students an opportunity to experience a wide variety of medical specialties. It also allows them to work with many different patients. As they gain knowledge about the different areas of medicine, most students make decisions about which field they like best.

Pediatrician Heather Burrows says that the clinical rotations are a wonderful chance for students to find out what being a doctor is really like. One of her most memorable experiences happened during her third year of medical school, when she was doing a rotation in OB/GYN. It was the middle of the night, and a woman was about to have a baby. Dr. Burrows describes the situation: "I was going to assist with the birth, and I was exhausted from working so many hours. All I wanted was for her to hurry up and get it over with so I could go to sleep. But then the baby was born . . . and it was the most amazing thing I've ever seen. All of a sudden, I was wide awake. I was so excited to be a part of this experience, helping to make this miracle happen."[2]

## Choosing a Specialty

Students continue their rotations during their fourth year of medical school, but they begin to take on more responsibility. Also, this is when they decide on their specialty. By their fourth year, they have had a chance to explore many different areas of medicine. They have seen real-life doctors in action, and they have worked alongside them. So the next step is to choose the medical field they want to pursue and

What It Takes to Be a Doctor • 19

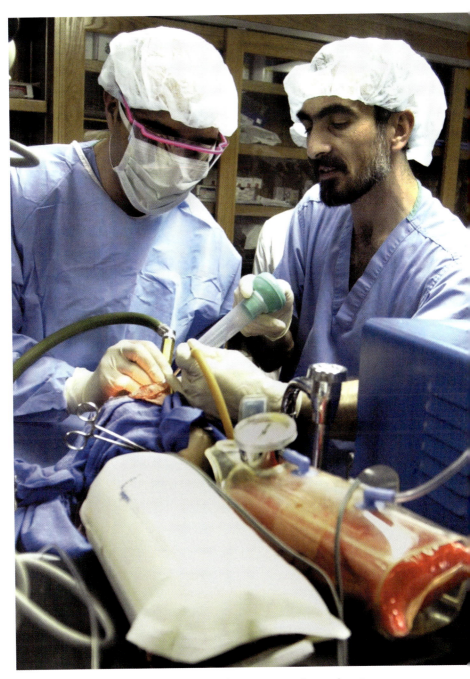

A doctor (right) teaches a student to perform brain surgery. By the fourth year of medical school, students choose their specialty.

graduate from medical school. Finally, they are officially doctors.

## Doctors-in-Training

By the time students graduate, they have completed eight years of formal schooling. However, their education is far from finished. Their next step is the **residency**, which is usually performed in a hospital under the direction of experienced physicians. A residency is an intense, hands-on medical training period that lasts for a minimum of three years. Some take much longer. For instance, residencies in anesthesiology and obstetrics take four years. An orthopedic surgery residency takes five years, and a plastic surgery residency takes six years. During this training period, residents are paid a salary for their work.

New doctors who are interested in a highly specialized field, such as neurosurgery, must perform residencies that last for six years or more. One example of this type of residency program is at Harborview Medical Center in Seattle. Dr. Richard Winn is the chief of neurosurgery, and he supervises the program. Each year, more than three hundred doctors apply—and only two are accepted. Plus, not only is the program hard to get into, it takes eight years to complete. A sign on Dr. Winn's office wall explains why his program is so difficult and why it takes such a long time. It reads, "If the training is tough, the war will be easy." Harborview's neurosurgical residency program has been called the best in the country.

Once doctors have completed their residencies, their formal medical training is finally complete. However, before they can practice medicine, they must get a license from the state in which they plan to work. When they are licensed, doctors may set up their own private practice or join a practice with other physicians. Or, they may go to work for hospitals, health departments, laboratories, or other medical organizations.

## What Makes a Good Doctor

Doctors work hard—very hard. Anyone who has put in the time and effort it takes to earn a medical degree is well aware of that. However, there are also other qualities that doctors need. First, they need to care about people. This applies to all doctors, even

A doctor examines X rays to determine what is wrong with her patient.

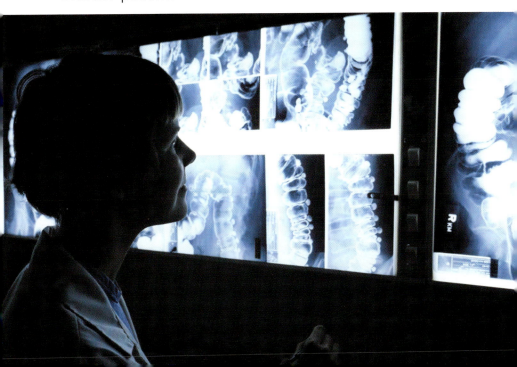

those who specialize in research or radiology. They may not work directly with patients, but their work still revolves around helping people. Doctors also need to be excellent thinkers. They must be able to examine a sick patient and figure out what is wrong. Then, they must be able to decide the best way to treat the patient's illness or injury.

## A Special Kind of Person

Dr. Dana Gossett is an OB/GYN who became a doctor for several reasons. She wanted to help people and to have a positive impact on their lives. But she also loves the science that is involved in medicine. She enjoys knowing how the body works and why disease happens. Dr. Gossett shares her thoughts about some qualities that doctors need: "Attention to detail is critical—little things can mean life or death in medicine. The physician MUST be able to listen—the patient frequently can tell you exactly what's wrong, if you can listen. And the physician must be [understanding]. If you can't place yourself in your patient's shoes and understand how scared/happy/painful/etc. their situation is, you will not be able to help them as much, and they will not trust you as much."[3]

It takes a special kind of person to be a doctor, and it is not the right career for everyone. However, for people with the right personal qualities—as well as the willingness to complete years of medical education and training—becoming a doctor is the best possible choice they could make.

CHAPTER 3

# What Doctors Do

How doctors spend their time depends on what type of physician they are and where they work. Some doctors work in hospitals, some work in offices, and some work in laboratories. Many work very long hours, from the early morning until well after dark. Others keep regular daytime office hours. In fact, the only thing that all doctors have in common is that no two days are ever exactly the same.

## The Children's Doctor

Dr. Burrows is in her third year of pediatric residency at the University of Michigan (U of M) Health System. She works six days per week, and one or two nights, at the hospital. A typical day at work begins at about 6:30 A.M. First, Dr. Burrows meets with the night shift doctors to find out what happened the night before. During her shift, she typically sees about fifteen to twenty patients per day. She visits with children and teenagers who suffer from such illnesses as asthma, pneumonia, and skin infections as well as a variety of other ailments. She also sees patients with different types of cancer and other life-threatening diseases. Since parents often have concerns about their children, she spends time meeting with them to answer any questions they may have.

In addition to working at the hospital, Dr. Burrows works one or two half-days per week at the U of M pediatric clinic. She explains how this differs from her work at the hospital:

> The kids who come into the clinic are there for more routine medical reasons, such as physicals and checkups. For instance, today at the clinic I saw two kids who had coughs, two with eye infections, one who was having a behavioral problem at school, a newborn baby who needed a six-week exam, and a boy who wanted a wart removed. This is very different from the hospital, where the patients I see are more seriously ill.[4]

## Helping Patients Relax

Dr. Burrows says that one of the things she enjoys most about working in pediatrics, both in the hospital and the clinic, is the relaxed atmosphere. She explains why this is important:

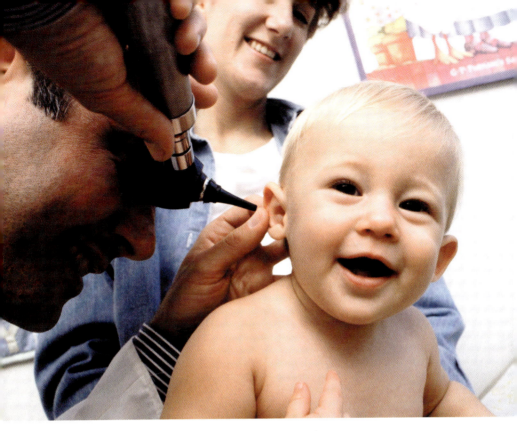

A pediatrician checks a baby's ears. Pediatricians must make children feel comfortable before examining them.

Children are scared when they come to see a doctor, and it's our job to help them relax. That's why doctors who work in pediatrics tend to be more laid back than doctors in other areas. We can't just start examining these kids without first making them feel comfortable with us. We need to gain their trust, to help them understand that it's going to be okay, that we're there to help them, not hurt them. That's why we rarely wear white coats, and the guys wear ties with cartoon characters on them. We all have goofy animals hanging off our stethoscopes, and we aren't afraid to get down on the floor and play with the kids. It's a way of helping them not be afraid. That is so important.[5]

## Caring for Families

Like pediatricians, family practice doctors spend their days seeing patients. However, their patients are not just children. Family practice doctors care for people of all different ages. Dr. James Cooke is a family practice doctor who finished his residency in 2000. He works in a medical practice along with several other physicians in Chelsea, Michigan.

A boy gets a checkup from his doctor. Family practice doctors care for children and adults.

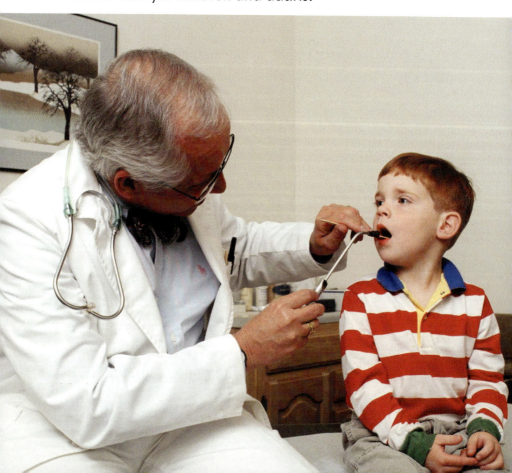

Dr. Cooke typically gets to work about 7:00 A.M. each day. The first thing he does is check his e-mail, because patients often send questions to him. He responds to them and then starts seeing patients. Between 8:00 A.M. and 5:00 P.M. he sees an average of twenty-five to thirty patients. People of all ages come to see him for many different reasons. For instance, parents bring their children in for physicals or because they are sick with sinus infections, ear infections, or the flu. Older adults come in with illnesses such as heart disease, diabetes, or high cholesterol. Pregnant women come in for regular prenatal visits and then later bring their babies in for checkups and vaccinations. Dr. Cooke spends time with these patients, examines them, and sometimes prescribes medicine or other treatments. Also, he performs minor surgeries in his office, such as freezing off warts, taking off bad toenails, or removing moles.

## Working in Hospitals

In addition to seeing patients in his office, Dr. Cooke also works in the hospital about six weeks out of the year. Plus, if one of his pregnant patients goes into labor, he may be called at any time of the day or night to deliver a baby.

Another aspect of Dr. Cooke's job is providing supervision to residents. He says he enjoys the teaching part of his job as much as he enjoys working with patients: "There are many reasons why I love being a doctor. I can help a lot of people, and taking care of patients is rewarding. But I also get a lot of satisfaction in helping new residents learn to be better doctors. At the end of each day, I feel good about the work I do."[6]

## Life of a Surgeon

A surgeon's job is quite different from that of a family practice doctor. Surgeons spend most of their time in hospitals, where they check on patients, meet with families, and perform surgery. Dr. Robert Shack works for a major hospital in New Jersey, and he has been a surgeon for twenty-six years. He is blunt when he describes what surgery is all about: "There is no such thing as a casual or routine surgery. If you think that, and a problem comes along, you are going to wish you were in another specialty very quickly. Every case is unique and different. . . . Surgery involves discipline. It does not matter if you had an argument with your wife or a tough night before, you are obligated to provide a professional product for your patient, and good doctors do."[7]

On one particular day, Dr. Shack performed operations on three patients. At 7:30 A.M. he performed gallbladder surgery on a female patient. At 10:30 A.M. he performed a mastectomy (breast removal) on a woman with breast cancer. At 12:30 P.M. he performed surgery on a man to repair a hernia. This was a complicated operation that took a long time to complete. In between and after the surgeries he reviewed laboratory reports, talked with patients and their families, and consulted with other physicians.

According to Dr. Shack, being a surgeon can be stressful. Even the best surgeons have a tough time if

What Doctors Do • 29

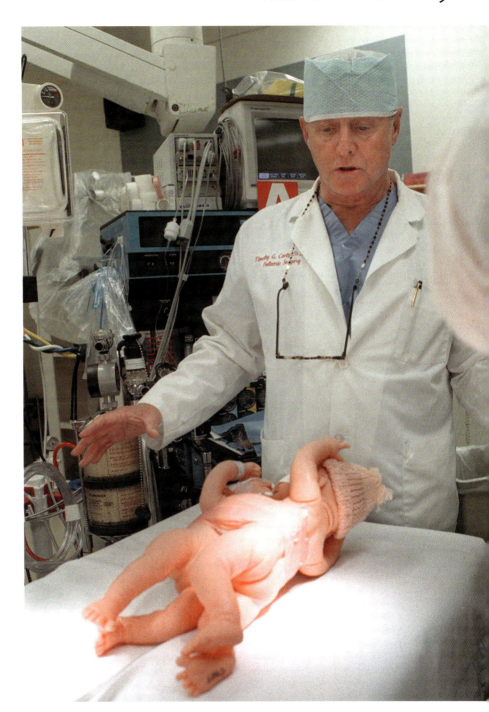

A surgeon uses dolls to demonstrate the complicated procedure he will use to separate Siamese twins.

they run into complications during surgery. If that happens, or if things go wrong, they must be able to learn from the experience. In spite of the difficulties of the profession, Dr. Shack finds being a surgeon to be extremely gratifying.

Surgeons sometimes wear special magnifying glasses and headlamps to help them see better while operating.

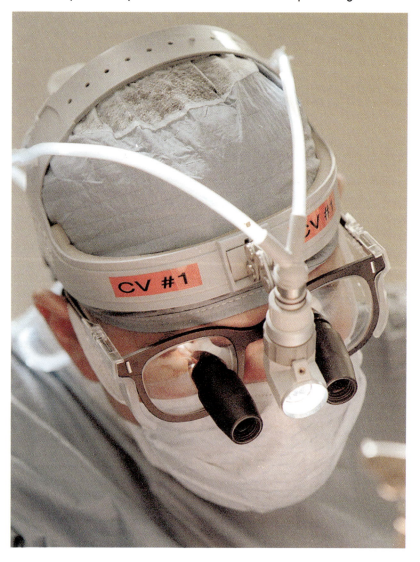

## The Role of the Anesthesiologist

Surgery is one area of medicine that requires different kinds of doctors to work together. During surgery, anesthesiologists play an important role. They provide pain relief and care to patients before, during, and after operations.

Doctors use different types of anesthesia based on what surgery patients are having. In some cases, anesthesiologists give an injection that deadens the nerves in just one area. Other times, patients need to be completely anesthetized—unconscious and unaware of pain. They receive this type of anesthetic either by breathing it through a mask or by an injection. Once a patient is asleep, the anesthesiologist controls the flow of air to the patient's lungs. For this reason the anesthesiologist must stay close by during surgery. He or she watches the patient's **vital signs** including blood pressure, heart rate, breathing, and temperature all through surgery. After surgery the patient is taken to a recovery room. In most cases, anesthesiologists determine when the anesthetic has worn off and patients are able to leave the recovery room.

No two doctors do exactly the same thing. In fact, if five doctors are asked to describe what they do from day to day, they will give five different answers. Yet, no matter how their work and tasks may differ, doctors' days are often long, and their work is often intense.

CHAPTER 4

# Meet a Doctor

Dr. Gerard Martin is a doctor in the emergency department at Henry Ford Hospital in Detroit. He has been a physician for over twenty years. In addition to being the senior staff doctor in the ER, he also supervises a staff of ER residents, nurses, and support professionals.

## How He Got His Start

Dr. Martin says that his dad was the one who encouraged him to think about becoming a doctor.

> My dad was a practical guy. He knew how much I liked science and math, and that I was good in those subjects. He suggested that I explore a premed program in college, and see how I liked it. Actually, I was a little scared of the idea. I knew that doctors had to talk to patients all the time—to touch them, to interact with them. I was pretty shy and didn't know

if I was the "doctor type." I just wasn't sure if it was the right career for me.[8]

His dad had a friend who was a pathologist, so Dr. Martin spent some time with him to see what his job was like. That is when he began to develop an interest in medicine, especially in pathology. "Pathologists don't have to spend much time with patients because most of their time is spent in the laboratory. I figured, this way I could have a job that used math and science, but being shy wouldn't matter."

Doctors wear protective face masks to keep germs from spreading to their patients.

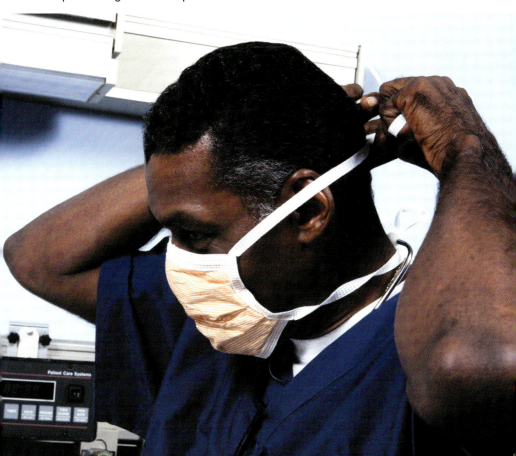

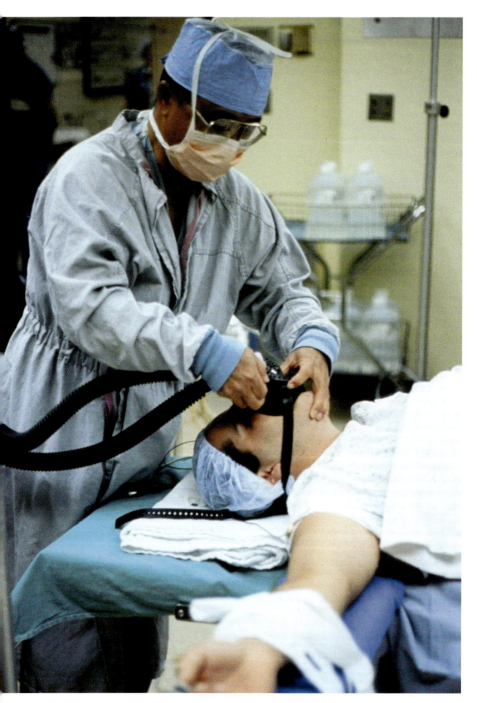

A surgeon places an oxygen mask on a patient to help him breathe better during an operation.

Dr. Martin finished a premed program in college and enrolled in St. Louis University Medical School. For the first two years, he studied all the typical medical school subjects. When he got into his third year, he began to think about other specialties besides pathology. "I wasn't that serious about pathology anyway, and as soon as I started having contact with patients, I found out how much I liked that part of it. I knew that whatever I chose, I wanted to deal closely with patients. However, the choices were immense. It's very common for medical students to feel torn when they start going through their rotations. I wanted to specialize in everything."

Of special interest to Dr. Martin was the field of pediatric heart surgery. During his rotations, he had the chance to work with a pediatric heart surgeon and was fascinated with the doctor's work.

> I spent a lot of time with him and I thought he was so great—I wanted to be just like him. To be able to help little kids who are born with heart defects seemed so incredible to me. What changed my mind was the hours this guy worked. I got there early in the morning, and he was always there before me. I left late at night, and he was always there after me. Those types of specialists work so many hours, it seems like they work all the time. I decided that I needed to choose something that allowed me a little more control over my life.

## Life in the ER

Emergency medicine first caught Dr. Martin's interest because it was so fast paced. Also, the field of emergency medicine had just become an official specialty about the time he graduated from medical school. "In years past, emergency medicine was not a specialty at all. In fact, the ER was viewed as not a very good place to work. Doctors would get stuck in there because they happened to be available. That changed during the 1970s, when emergency medicine started to be more recognized. I talked to people in the field, and decided it might be the right choice for me." After he graduated from medical school, Dr. Martin went to work at Henry Ford Hospital. He has been there ever since.

A surgeon prepares to make an incision during an operation.

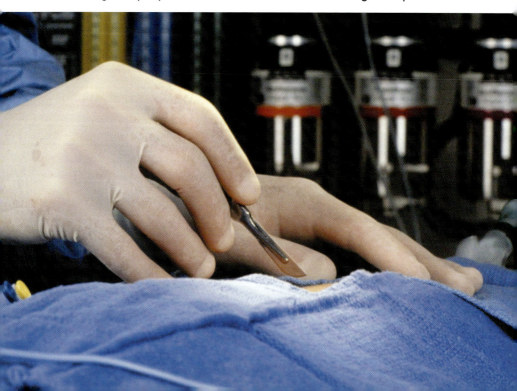

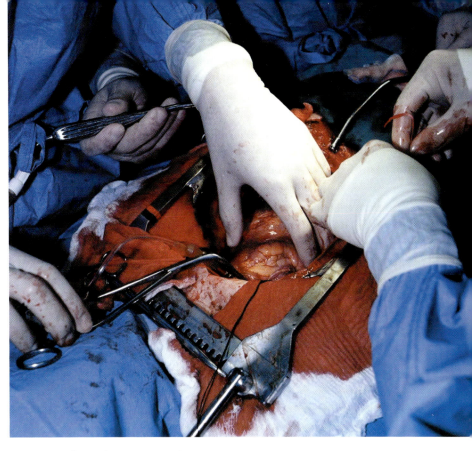

A team of ER doctors performs emergency surgery.

Dr. Martin says that real-life emergency rooms are not exactly like those shown on television, although there are similarities. In a real ER things are very fast paced, so doctors and nurses do not have time to stand around and chat the way they do on television. Also, television shows tend to feature only the most dramatic injuries and illnesses. "We do get our share of those cases in the ER. We see shooting victims and people who have suffered heart attacks or overdosed on drugs. But we also get plenty of sprained ankles, bellyaches, slivers in fingers, and tons of other stuff that wouldn't be exciting enough to show on TV."

The Henry Ford ER staff works three shifts a day, so the ER is covered twenty-four hours a day, seven days a week. Dr. Martin has been there for a long time, but he works his share of afternoons and nights just like everyone else. He says that it is a very, very busy place. "Sometimes we see nearly three hundred patients in a day, so it can get hectic. We all work hard."

## Best Things About the Job

Dr. Martin loves the fact that in the ER, everyone expects the unexpected.

> We never know who will come in the door or what will be wrong with them. And we see it all—heart attacks, gunshot wounds, sore throats, splinters in fingers, seizures, car accident victims—everything from the most minor thing to the worst thing you could imagine. Often, we are able to help these people and save their lives.
>
> One particular case involved a young man who had been at a party with his buddies. A fight broke out and he was stabbed in the chest, which resulted in a stab wound to his heart. When he was brought into the ER, he was gasping for breath. Blood had accumulated around his heart and that was preventing it from beating properly. We opened his chest, removed the blood from around his heart, and got his heartbeat back under con-

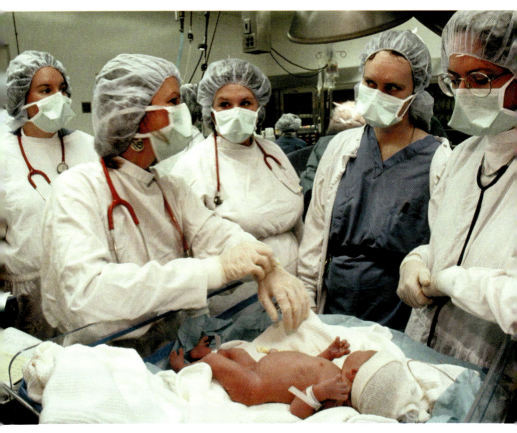

Doctors examine a newborn baby. Delivering babies is just one of the many satisfying parts of a doctor's job.

trol. His chances for survival hadn't been very good, yet he fully recovered and was able to go back to college. Our team saved his life, and I can't even begin to describe what that feels like.

Dr. Martin says he also enjoys the teaching part of his job. "I find it very satisfying to play a part in our residents' development, to help them learn. I have the opportunity to help them make the transition from knowing nothing to being good doctors."

## The Bad Times

As with any job, life in the ER is not always pleasant. The fast pace can be exciting, but it can also be exhausting. Plus, there are tragedies.

> We see some really bad situations. Cases where babies have been shaken and they're brain damaged. Victims of car accidents or stab wounds. Child abuse. People who have been beaten. The hardest times, of course, are when people die. One of our saddest cases involved an older gentleman named "Albert." He had been in the ER countless times because he was quite a drinker, and he would end up getting hurt. He came in so much that he kind of got on our nerves, because sometimes he could be obnoxious. Then one day an ambulance arrived with a man who had been hit by a car and was badly hurt. He died shortly after he got there, and after he died, we realized it was Albert. We couldn't believe it. After years of taking care of this guy—even though we'd been irritated at him sometimes—his death hit us all really hard. We were pretty broken up for a while because of that.

## Message to Kids

Dr. Martin believes that being a doctor is a great career for the right person. He says that because of all the different fields and specialties, there is something for almost everyone. "If you want lots of patient contact, go to work in the ER or family practice. If you don't want contact with patients, be a pathologist. If you love kids, be a pediatrician. No matter what area you choose, you can make some kind of positive difference." He cautions, however, that aspiring doctors must look at a medical career realistically. "It takes a long time and a lot of work to become a doctor. Plus, once you do, the hours are long and the work isn't easy. But I believe it's well worth it. Being a doctor is both rewarding and challenging. My job is to help people in their time of need. I can't think of anything better than that."

# NOTES

## Chapter 1: Different Kinds of Doctors
1. Quoted in Lelia Gray, "Town & Country," University of Washington, September 1998. www.washington.edu.

## Chapter 2: What It Takes to Be a Doctor
2. Dr. Heather Burrows, interview with author, September 26, 2002.
3. Quoted in *Students Science Enrichment Program (SSEP),* "Dr. Dana Gossett." http://ssep.bwfund.org.

## Chapter 3: What Doctors Do
4. Burrows, interview with author.
5. Burrows, interview with author.
6. Dr. James Cooke, interview with author, September 26, 2002.
7. Quoted in Beth Salamon, "A Day in the Life of a Surgeon," *Family Health.* Saint Barnabas Health Care System, Spring/Summer 2001.

## Chapter 4: Meet a Doctor
8. All quotes in Chapter 4: Dr. Gerard Martin, interview with author, September 13, 2002.

# GLOSSARY

**anesthesiologist:** A medical doctor who administers anesthesia during surgery.

**CAT scan (computerized axial tomography):** A picture of the body's internal parts, using a combination of computer and X rays.

**dermatologist:** A doctor who specializes in diagnosing diseases of the skin, hair, and nails.

**epidemiologist:** A doctor who studies how many people contract an illness, how it spreads, and its origins.

**hematologist:** A doctor who specializes in treating diseases of the blood such as anemia and leukemia.

**immune system:** The body's system of organs and cells that defend it against infection, disease, and foreign substances.

**internist:** An internal medicine doctor who specializes in diagnosis and treatment of illness in adults.

**magnetic resonance imaging (MRI):** A diagnostic procedure that takes pictures of the body.

**neurosurgeon:** A surgeon who specializes in the brain, spinal cord, and nerves.

**obstetrician:** A doctor who specializes in pregnant women and the delivery of babies.

**oncologist:** A doctor who specializes in treating cancer.

**ophthalmologist:** A doctor who specializes in the diagnosis and treatment of eye diseases.

**orthopedic surgeon:** A doctor who operates on bones, joints, muscles, nerves, and tendons.

**otolaryngologist:** A doctor who specializes in ear, nose, and throat disorders.

**pathologist:** A doctor who analyzes human cells and tissue to determine diseases and conditions; a forensic pathologist performs autopsies to determine cause of death.

**pediatrician:** A doctor who specializes in treating children, from babies to teenagers.

**pediatric surgeon:** A surgeon who specializes in performing surgeries on children.

**plastic surgeon:** A doctor who uses surgery to repair the function or appearance of body parts.

**radiologist:** A doctor who interprets X rays and other diagnostic tests.

**residency:** An on-the-job training program that prepares medical school graduates for careers as doctors.

**surgeon:** A doctor who performs operations.

**vital signs:** Blood pressure, pulse, heart rate, and temperature.

# FOR FURTHER EXPLORATION

### Books
Clinton Cox, *African American Healers.* New York: John Wiley & Sons, 2000. Profiles over thirty African Americans who have made significant contributions in medicine.

Lucile Davis, *The Mayo Brothers: Doctors to the World.* New York: Childrens Press, 1998. A biography of the world-famous doctors who established the Mayo Clinic in Rochester, Minnesota.

Francene Sabin, *Elizabeth Blackwell, the First Woman Doctor.* Mahwah, NJ: Troll Associates, 1982. Traces the early life of the first woman physician and describes the struggle women had to face in becoming doctors and practicing medicine.

Jill C. Wheeler, *E.R. Doctors.* Edina, MN: Abdo, 2002. Provides an inside look at life in the emergency room, including the doctors who work there.

Samuel G. Woods, *Pediatrician.* Woodbridge, CT: Blackbirch, 1999. A personal look at the career of Dr. Ron Angoff, a pediatrician.

### Periodical
Carol Blackburn, "Exploring Career Options: Oncologist," *IMAGINE,* May/June 1996. An interesting article about Dr. Bert Vogelstein, an oncologist who is one of the country's leading cancer researchers.

## Internet Sources

Carl Bianco, M.D. "How Becoming a Doctor Works," *How Stuff Works*. www.howstuffworks.com. Written by an emergency room doctor who provides interesting information about how people become doctors.

———, "How Emergency Rooms Work," *How Stuff Works*. www.howstuffworks.com. A very good explanation of what goes on in a hospital emergency room, written by an ER doctor.

Lelia Gray, "Town & Country," University of Washington, September 1998. www.washington.edu. An interesting article about rural doctors, with information about programs in rural medicine.

Eugenie Heitmiller, "How Anesthesia Works," *How Stuff Works*. www.howstuffworks.com. An informative write-up about what anesthesiologists do for patients.

*Students Science Enrichment Program (SSEP),* "Dr. Dana Gossett." http.//ssep.bwfund.org. An interview with a doctor who talks about why she decided on a medical career, why she became an obstetrician, and what her job is like.

*U.S. Bureau of Labor Statistics,* "Jobs for Kids Who Like . . . Science," March 28, 2002. www.bls.gov. An article about doctors: what they do, what their jobs are like, and how they prepare for a medical career.

# INDEX

Albert, 40
anesthesiologists, 10, 20, 31
autopsies, 10

Burrows, Heather, 18, 23–26

clinical rotations, 17–18, 35
college, 15–17
Cooke, James, 26–28
cosmetic surgery, 8
country doctors, 5–6
Curtis, Larry, 5–6

diagnostic tests, 10
disease detectives. *See*
  epidemiologists
doctors
  number of, 4
  qualities needed by, 21–22,
    25
  reasons for becoming, 14,
    32–33, 41
doctor's doctor. *See*
  pathologist

education and training
  choosing specialties during,
    33, 35–36
  college, 15–17
  length of, 14
  medical schools for, 16–18,
    20
  residencies as, 20–21, 23–26,
    27–28
emergency room (ER) doctors
  development as specialty,
    36
  flying by, 6–7
  workday of, 6, 37–40
epidemiologists, 13

family practice doctors, 4–6,
  26–28
forensic pathologists, 10

Gossett, Dana, 22

Harborview Medical Center,
  20
hematologists, 9
Henry Ford Hospital, 32, 36,
  38

internists, 9

47

Karl, Tom, 9

licenses, 21

Martin, Gerald
  choice of specialty by, 33, 35–36
  reasons for, becoming a doctor, 32–33
  workday of, 37–40
Medical College Admission Test (MCAT), 17
medical schools, 16–18, 20

neurosurgeons, 8, 20
obstetricians (OB/GYNs), 9, 20
oncologists, 10
ophthalmologists, 9
orthopedic surgeons, 8, 20
otolaryngolists, 9

pathologist, 10, 33
pediatricians, 9, 23–26
pediatric surgeons, 8–9
physicians. *See* doctors
plastic surgeons, 8, 20
premed, 15–17
primary care doctors, 4–6, 26–28

radiologists, 10

residencies. *See* education and training
rotations, 17–18, 35
rural doctors, 5–6

Shack, Robert, 28, 30–31
specialties
  clinical rotations and, 17–18, 35
  decision about, 18, 20, 33, 35–36
  length of residencies for, 20
  *see also names of specific specialties*
surgeons
  general, 7–8, 28, 30
  neurosurgeons, 8, 20
  orthopedic, 8, 20
  pediatric, 8–9
  plastic, 8, 20

training and education. *See* education and training

UCSF Children's Hospital, 9

vital signs, 31

Wimm, Richard, 20
workplaces, 21, 23